W8-BKG-826

This Book Belongs To:

_____

Zanders Portal
Created by Kurt Reetz

All Rights Reserved

No part of this book may be reproduced or transmitted in any form or by any means, electronic or mechanical, including photocopying, recording, or by any information storage or retrieval system, without written permission from the publisher

For more information visit:
www.shortmountains.com

Printed in the United States of America

ISBN: 979-8351577685

Senior Art Director Brian Fisher

"Zanders Portal" and all Short Mountains, LLC books are registered and copyrighted with the United States Copyright Office.
All Short Mountains, LLC digital content and products are registered, owned, and protected worldwide.

©Short Mountains, LLC 2022

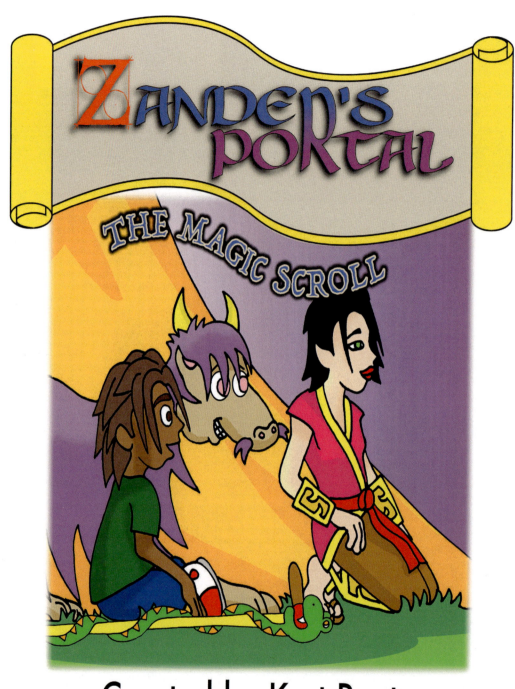

Created by Kurt Reetz
Written by Sondra Sula
Illustrated by Adam Chang

One rainy Sunday afternoon, Zander sat in his attic bedroom trying to put together a puzzle. All he needed was one last piece to complete the puzzle, but he couldn't find it. "Where did it go?" he wondered.

Zander saw the puzzle piece stuck between the floorboards. As he pulled on it, the floorboard popped up. He was surprised at what he found.

There was a large paper scroll hidden under the floor. "Wow, I wonder what it says," he thought. He pulled open the scroll and saw strange words written on it: "Kazooy changis daman kangarooy."

All of a sudden there was a bright light and a swirling tunnel formed right in front of him. Without warning, Zander was pulled into the tunnel.

Seconds later, Zander was in a forest with trees so tall he couldn't see the tops. Spongy moss covered the ground.

From out of nowhere a girl appeared and grabbed his hand. "Follow me! We've got to hide!" she said. She dragged Zander along the ground. The girl was very strong and wore strange clothing.

"Hey what are you doing?" Zander asked.
"Quiet! My name is Arra. Trust me," she whispered.
They hid together behind a rock.

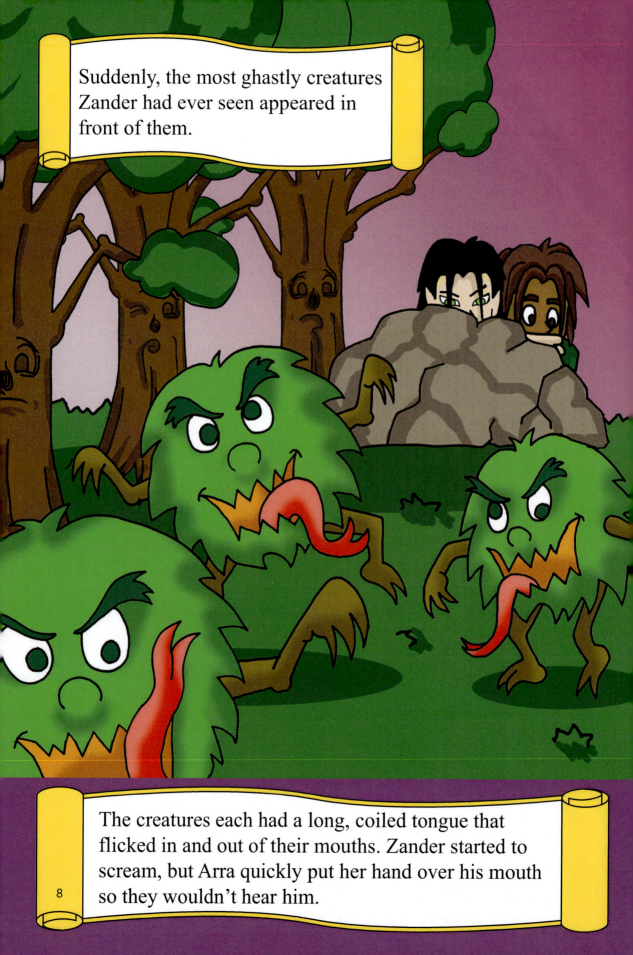

"Those are Trogs," Arra said.
Before Zander had time to think, a large beast jumped from behind a huge tree and frightened the Trogs away.
"Purryak!" Arra said, before Zander could ask.

"Thanks!" Arra shouted to Purryak as she popped up from behind the rock. Arra turned to Zander and said, "This is... what's your name, anyway?"

"My name is Zander."
"I am Purryak," the beast said, stretching out a hoof-like hand to Zander, who reluctantly shook it.

Arra and Purryak came to a halt in front of a large tree.

Something that looked like a small cucumber was sticking out of the tree. It appeared to be a sort of handle. Arra turned it and a hidden red door appeared. She turned the handle more and the door opened.

Inside was a rocking chair covered in jewels. Upon it sat a large mushroom, drinking a cup of tea and reading an old, worn spell book. "Oh, how do you do, Zander?" the mushroom said. "I am Gavin the Wizard."

"How do you know my name?" Zander asked.
"I know many things," Gavin said. "For example, I know that you were brought here to break the spell that turned me into a mushroom."

"Me?" asked Zander. "You will have help from Arra and Purryak, and from this." Gavin pulled out a gold scepter that looked like a coiled snake. Zander thought he saw one of the emerald eyes wink at him.

As soon as Zander held the scepter, everyone but the mushroom wizard was transported to a place far away from the forest.

They were surrounded by deep canyons and carved bridges. "How will we know what to do?" Zander asked.

"Gavin the Wizard will speak to your mind," Arra and Purryak said at the same time. "Then Zander heard a voice in his head say, talk to the Owlvark."

Zander felt someone, or something, staring at him. He turned around.

Big, pink eyes blinked. A voice came from a yellow beak. "Find the Parrotfish that lives in the lagoon. She will guide you," the voice said.

They quickly found the lagoon, and a bridge that went across it.

In the water below, Zander saw a bright fish swimming. The fish jumped out of the water and began to fly slowly in front of them.

"I am the Parrotfish. Follow me," she said.

They walked over several narrow brigdes following the Parrotfish. On one bridge, Purryak lost his footing and fell down toward the canyon below!

Without hesitation, Zander extended the snake scepter. It turned into a long rope that shot out and caught Purryak!

He was shaking with fear when Zander pulled him back up to the bridge. "Thanks for saving me, Zander," he said. Once again, the snake winked at Zander.

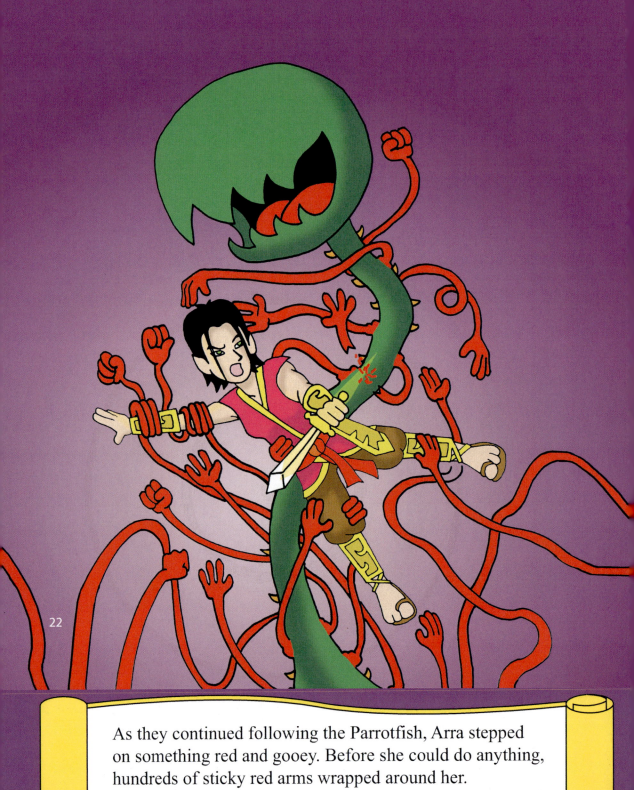

As they continued following the Parrotfish, Arra stepped on something red and gooey. Before she could do anything, hundreds of sticky red arms wrapped around her. She was trapped!

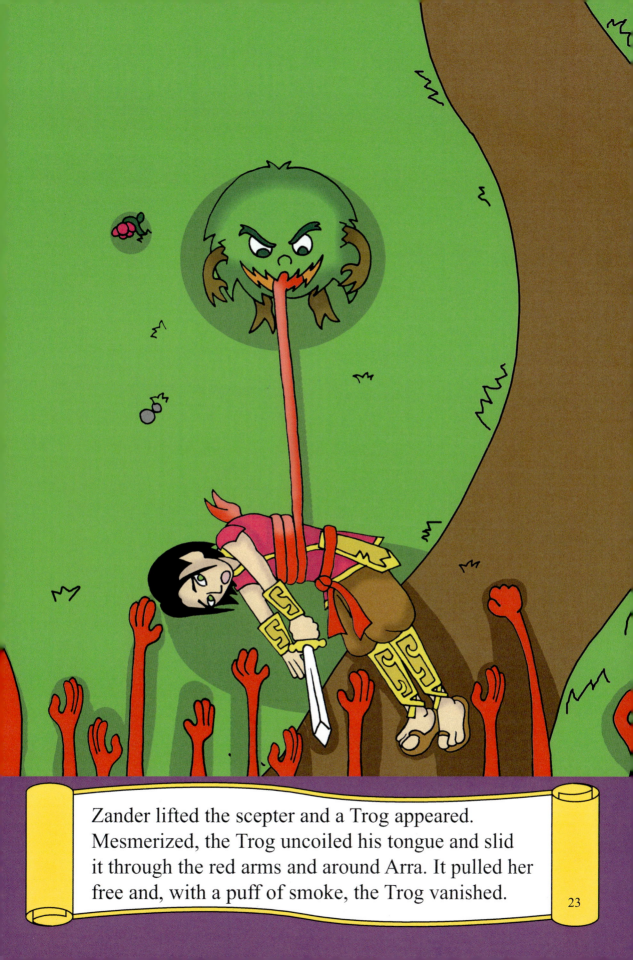

Zander lifted the scepter and a Trog appeared. Mesmerized, the Trog uncoiled his tongue and slid it through the red arms and around Arra. It pulled her free and, with a puff of smoke, the Trog vanished.

"I thought the Trogs were your enemies," Zander said. "They are," Purryak replied. "But the snake scepter turns what is bad into good. At least temporarily." Soon their travels brought them to a vast desert.

Then the Parrotfish spoke "My part of the journey ends here. Wait for the Ferrouche." The Parrotfish flew off.

Not long after, a creature that resembled a long, silver panther slithered down from a cliff above them. "I am the Ferrouche," it said. "I will take you to Crustbungler the Hag."

At an incredible speed, the Ferrouche carried the friends across the entire desert on his back and soon reached the home of Crustbungler the hag. They thanked him for his help and Zander approached the hags hut.

Crustbungler the Hag lived in an old toadstool with her pet vulture.

Zander heard Gavin's voice in his head again. It told him to snatch the magic ring off her finger to break the spell she placed on Gavin.
"What a lovely ring," Zander said sweetly.

"Oh, my," Crustbungler said. "Why, thank you, young man." She held her hand out so Zander could get a closer look.

The snake leapt off the scepter and stole the ring right off the hag's finger. As the hag shrieked, Zander and his friends were instantly transported back to Gavin the Wizard's hut.

Zander handed the ring back to the mushroom shaped wizard.

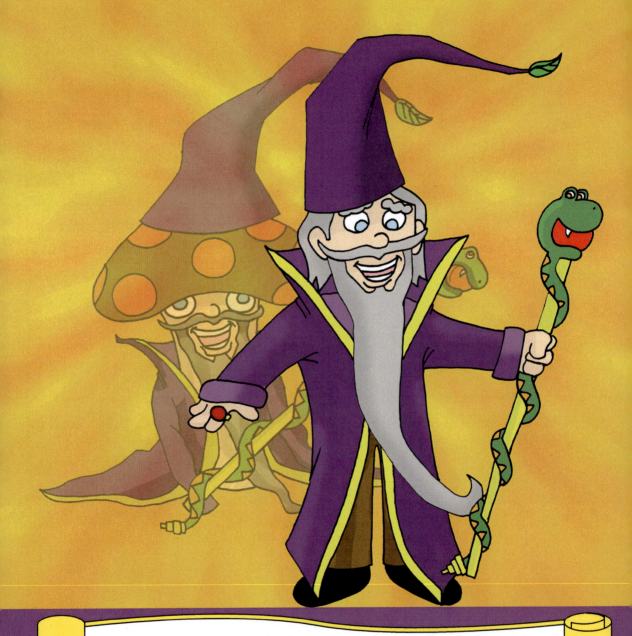

As he took it, Gavin began to change back into his true form. "I do not know what I would have done without your help, Zander," Gavin said. "I believe it's time to get you back home."

Purryak and Arra waved goodbye to Zander. "We hope you will return to our realm soon, brave Zander!" they cried. "I certainly will," Zander said. Then, with a wave of Gavin's snake scepter, Zander was gone.

Zander found himself back in his bedroom.
He placed the scroll underneath his bed to hide it.
He was so excited, he couldn't wait to go on another adventure with his new friends.